Dear Parents:

Congratulations! Your child is taking the first steps on an exciting journey. The destination? Independent reading!

STEP INTO READING® will help your child get there. The program offers five steps to reading success. Each step includes fun stories and colorful art or photographs. In addition to original fiction and books with favorite characters, there are Step into Reading Non-Fiction Readers, Phonics Readers and Boxed Sets, Sticker Readers, and Comic Readers—a complete literacy program with something to interest every child.

Learning to Read, Step by Step!

Ready to Read   Preschool–Kindergarten
• big type and easy words • rhyme and rhythm • picture clues
For children who know the alphabet and are eager to begin reading.

Reading with Help   Preschool–Grade 1
• basic vocabulary • short sentences • simple stories
For children who recognize familiar words and sound out new words with help.

Reading on Your Own   Grades 1–3
• engaging characters • easy-to-follow plots • popular topics
For children who are ready to read on their own.

Reading Paragraphs   Grades 2–3
• challenging vocabulary • short paragraphs • exciting stories
For newly independent readers who read simple sentences with confidence.

Ready for Chapters   Grades 2–4
• chapters • longer paragraphs • full-color art
For children who want to take the plunge into chapter books but still like colorful pictures.

STEP INTO READING® is designed to give every child a successful reading experience. The grade levels are only guides; children will progress through the steps at their own speed, developing confidence in their reading.

Remember, a lifetime love of reading starts with a single step!

For Grandma
–K.D.

Copyright © 2016 Disney Enterprises, Inc. All rights reserved. Published in the United States by Random House Children's Books, a division of Penguin Random House LLC, 1745 Broadway, New York, NY 10019, and in Canada by Random House of Canada, a division of Penguin Random House Ltd., Toronto, in conjunction with Disney Enterprises, Inc.

Step into Reading, Random House, and the Random House colophon are registered trademarks of Penguin Random House LLC.

Visit us on the Web!
StepIntoReading.com
randomhousekids.com

Educators and librarians, for a variety of teaching tools, visit us at RHTeachersLibrarians.com

ISBN 978-0-7364-3452-2 (trade) — ISBN 978-0-7364-8213-4 (lib. bdg.)
ISBN 978-0-7364-3453-9 (ebook)

Printed in the United States of America
10 9 8 7 6 5 4 3 2 1

A Royal Spring

by Kristen Depken
illustrated by Fabio Laguna
and Marco Colletti

Random House 🏠 New York

Rapunzel

It is spring!
Time to get ready
for Easter.

Rapunzel and Pascal
color Easter eggs.
Pascal gathers eggs.
Rapunzel makes dye.

Rapunzel paints
so many eggs!
Pascal helps.

Rapunzel and Pascal
put the eggs in baskets.
They are ready
for Easter!

Tiana

Tiana is having
a garden party!
She hangs flowers.

Naveen sets up tables.
Louis sets the stage
for the band.

It is party time!
Tiana serves gumbo
and sweet treats.

The band plays.

Everyone dances.

It is the perfect
garden party!

Belle

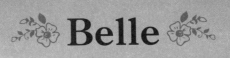

Belle's flowers are
in bloom!

Belle trims the roses.

Snip, snip!

Belle puts a blanket
on the grass.
She takes yummy food
out of a picnic basket.

Belle's picnic is ready.
Everyone eats
tasty treats.

The Prince helps Chip
fly a kite.
What a lovely day!

Merida

Merida and Angus go
for a ride.

They see a rainbow!

Angus stops
for a drink of water.
Merida finds
a lost baby bunny!

Merida and Angus look

for the bunny's family.

They ride deep

into the forest.

Merida looks
in the bushes.
No bunnies!

Merida and Angus
find a clearing.
It is full of animals.

The baby bunny
finds his family.
Hooray!

Spring is so much fun!

1-16